SPORK

Written by **Kyo Maclear**

Illustrated by **Isabelle Arsenault**

KIDS CAN PRESS

Spork was neither spoon nor fork ...

spoon

fork

Spork

... but a bit of **both**.

He had a **mum** and a **dad** …

... who both thought he was perfect
just the way he was.

But **Spork** stuck out.

In his kitchen, forks were forks and
spoons were spoons. Cutlery customs were
followed closely. Mixing was uncommon.
Naturally, there were rule breakers: knives
who loved chopsticks, tongs who married forks.
But such families were unusual.

One day, after the billionth time he was asked "What are you, anyway?" and the zillionth time he was passed over when the table was being set …

… Spork sighed and thought, "It must be easier to be a single thing." And he decided he'd try to pick just ONE thing to be.

He thought he should start by fixing

his head. He put on a bowler hat to look

more spoonish. But the forks

thought he was too round.

Then he made a paper crown to look **more forkish**. But the spoons thought he was too pointy.

Spork wondered if there were other lonely creatures out
there with **no matching kind**, who never got
chosen to be at the table.

At dinnertime, he watched from the drawer
while the spoons played pea hockey and skillfully balanced boiled
eggs. He sat off to the side while the forks raked fancy patterns in
the mashed potatoes and twirled noodles around in complicated
circles like rhythmic gymnasts. And at the end of this and every
other meal, Spork looked on while the
others enjoyed a super-bubbly
bath in the sink.

Until one morning, a **messy thing** arrived.
This messy thing had obviously never heard of cutlery
customs or table manners. No. This messy thing smeared and
spilled and flung and clumped and dripped without a care.

"Wait!" said the forks.

But the messy thing did not wait.

"Careful!"

said the spoons. But the messy

thing was not careful.

"Help!" said the forks
while the messy thing continued to
slop and splatter.

"Quick!"
said the spoons.

Now, a fork may be good for poking and picking.

And a spoon may be fine for scooping and stirring.

But this messy thing with its slurpy and clumpy
half-finished food bits needed **something else**.
Something that could do all sorts of things at once.
Something flexible and easy to hold.

Something that was neither
spoon nor fork but a
bit of both.

That's when **Spork** landed.

The messy thing saw Spork and immediately

stopped. And gurgled.

It grabbed Spork and held him motionless in its fist.

It tapped him once and let out a cheerful shriek.

It wagged Spork excitedly up and down.

And that's how **Spork** finally and happily found his way to the table.

Just a bit round. Just a bit pointy.

Just right.

To Yoshi and Mika (my sons), David (cocreator),
Tara–Isabelle–Karen (dream team) and to all the
amazing sporks and misfits in my life — K.M.

To Arnaud and Florent, my two messy things,
and to Fred, who helps me handle their everyday
splashes! Love you all — I.A.

Text © 2010 Kyo Maclear
Illustrations © 2010 Isabelle Arsenault

Kids Can Press acknowledges the financial support of
the Government of Ontario, through the Ontario Media
Development Corporation's Ontario Book Initiative; the
Ontario Arts Council; the Canada Council for the Arts; and
the Government of Canada, through the BPIDP, for our
publishing activity.

Published in Canada by   Published in the U.S. by
Kids Can Press Ltd.   Kids Can Press Ltd.
25 Dockside Drive   2250 Military Road
Toronto, ON M5A 0B5   Tonawanda, NY 14150

www.kidscanpress.com

Kids Can Press is a *Corus*™ Entertainment company

The artwork in this book was rendered in
mixed media and assembled digitally.
The text is set in Clarendon Light.

Edited by Tara Walker
Designed by Karen Powers

This book is smyth sewn casebound.
Manufactured in Altona, Manitoba,
Canada, in 11/2010 by Friesens Corporation

CM 10 0 9 8 7 6 5 4 3 2

**Library and Archives Canada Cataloguing
in Publication**

Maclear, Kyo Iona, 1970–
    Spork / written by Kyo Maclear;
illustrated by Isabelle Arsenault.

ISBN 978-1-55337-736-8

I. Arsenault, Isabelle, 1978– II. Title.

PS8625.L435S66 2010   jC813'.6
C2010-900440-X